For Lon,
who loves those babies,
ducks, and me

A. H.

For my three heroines and a hero—
Amelia, Helen, Lucy, and David

J. B.

Text copyright © 1996 by Amy Hest
Illustrations copyright © 1996 by Jill Barton

All rights reserved.

First U.S. edition 1996

Library of Congress Cataloging-in-Publication Data

Hest, Amy.
Baby Duck and the bad eyeglasses / Amy Hest ;
illustrated by Jill Barton.—1st ed.
Sequel to: In the rain with Baby Duck.
Summary: Baby Duck is unhappy about the new eyeglasses she has to
wear, until Grampa helps her realize that they are not so bad after all.
ISBN 1-56402-680-9
[1. Ducks—Fiction. 2. Eyeglasses—Fiction. 3. Grandfathers—Fiction.]
I. Barton, Jill, ill. II. Title.
PZ7.H4375Bab   1996
[E]—dc20   95-33662

2 4 6 8 10 9 7 5 3 1

Printed in Italy

This book was typeset in Opti Lucius Bold.
The pictures were done in pencil and watercolor.

Candlewick Press
2067 Massachusetts Avenue
Cambridge, Massachusetts 02140

Baby Duck
and the
Bad Eyeglasses

Amy Hest

illustrated by Jill Barton

CANDLEWICK PRESS
CAMBRIDGE, MASSACHUSETTS

Baby Duck was looking in the mirror.

She was sizing up her new eyeglasses.

They were too big on her baby face.

They pushed against her baby cheeks.

And, she did not look like Baby.

Baby came slowly down the stairs.
"Park time!" said Mr. Duck. "Grampa
will be waiting in his boat at the lake!"
"How sweet you look in your
new eyeglasses!" cooed Mrs. Duck.
"Don't you love them?"

"No," Baby said.

"How well you must see in your new eyeglasses!" clucked Mr. Duck.

"Don't you like them just a little?"

"No," Baby said.

The Duck family filed out the front door.

Mr. and Mrs. Duck hopped along.

"Hop down the lane, Baby!"

Baby did not hop. Her glasses

might fall off.

Mr. and Mrs. Duck danced along.

"Dance down the lane, Baby!"

Baby did not dance.

Her glasses might fall off.

When they got to the park, Baby sat in the grass behind a tree. She sang a little song.

"Poor, poor Baby, she looks ugly
In her bad eyeglasses.
Everyone can play but me,
Poor, poor, poor, poor Baby . . ."

Grampa came up the hill.

"Where's that Baby?" he called.

"I'm afraid she is hiding." Mrs. Duck sighed.

"She does not like her new eyeglasses,"
worried Mr. Duck.

Grampa sat in the grass behind the tree.

"I like your hiding place," he whispered.

"Thank you," Baby said.

Grampa peeked around the side of the tree.

"I see new eyeglasses," he whispered. "Are they blue?"

"No," Baby said.

"Green?" Grampa whispered.

"No," Baby said.

"Cocoa brown?"

Grampa whispered.

Baby came out from behind the tree. Grampa folded his arms. "Well," he said, "I think those eyeglasses are very fine."

"Why?" Baby asked.

"Because they are red like mine," Grampa said.

Grampa kissed Baby's cheek. "Can you still run into the lake and splash around?"

Baby ran and splashed.

Then she
splashed harder.

Her glasses
did not fall off.

"Can you still twirl three times without falling down?"

Baby twirled.

One,

two,

three.

She did not fall down.
And her glasses did
not fall off.

"Come with me, Baby.

I have a surprise," Grampa said.

They walked down to the pier.
Grampa's boat was bobbing on the
water. There was another boat, too.
"Can you read what it says?"
Grampa asked.
Baby read, "B-a-b-y."
The letters were very clear.

Then Grampa and Mr. and Mrs. Duck
sat in Grampa's boat. But Baby sat in
her boat and she sang a new song.

"I have nice new eyeglasses;
I look like my Grampa.
My rowboat is lots of fun,
And I can read my name on it . . ."